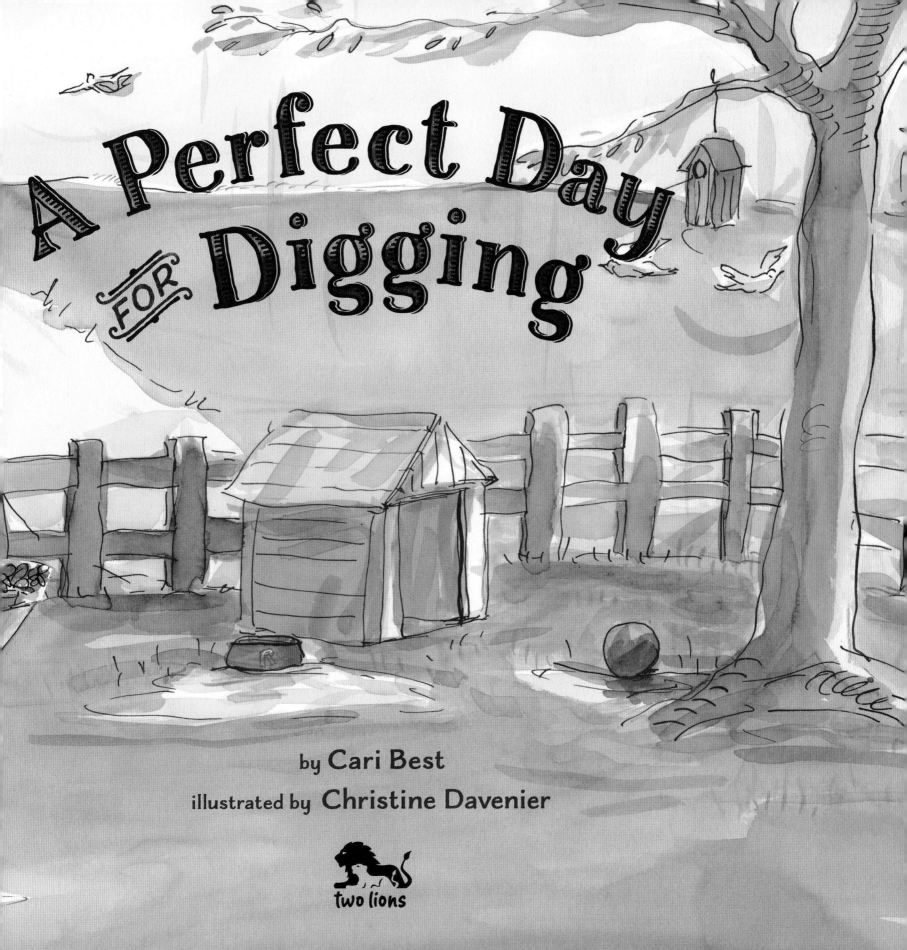

A Perfect Day for Digging

by Cari Best

illustrated by Christine Davenier

two lions

For lovers of the good earth
—C.B.

For Babo and Marcel to celebrate their love
—C.D.

two lions

Text copyright © 2014 by Cari Best
Illustrations copyright © 2014 by Christine Davenier
All rights reserved

Amazon Publishing
Attn: Amazon Children's Publishing
P.O. Box 400818
Las Vegas, NV 89140
www.amazon.com/amazonchildrenspublishing

Library of Congress Cataloging-in-Publication Data is available upon request.

ISBN-13: 9781477847060 (hardcover)
ISBN-10: 1477847065 (hardcover)
ISBN-13: 9781477897065 (eBook)
ISBN-10: 1477897062 (eBook)

The illustrations are rendered in ink and pencil on watercolor paper.
Interior Book Design by Virginia Pope
Editor: Melanie Kroupa

Printed in China (R)
First edition

In the spring when trees unfreeze and grass grows green
and pansies say, "Please plant me," Nell and Rusty can't wait
to dig in dirt just right for digging.

"Bye, bye, snow shovel," says Nell. "Hello, trowel!"

Crunch!

Crumble!

Push!

Shove!

Victory!

"Victory!" Nell sings when she and Rusty finally break through the crusty ground.

"I love the smell of fresh spring dirt," Nell says. "Don't you, Rusty?"

Rusty does. In fact, he loves the smell of fresh spring dirt so much that he tries to eat it.

Then Nell has to remind him:

"Dirt is for digging, Rusty, not eating."

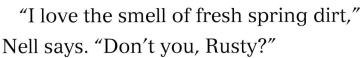

Nell swirls the dirt around making
s's with her trowel.

She chip-chops the clumpy, lumpy
dirt until it is silky smooth.

Rusty makes dirt angels.

Then he jumps up and shakes.

"Hooray for getting dirty!" shouts Nell.

"Woof!" barks Rusty.

"I hate getting dirty," says Norman,
swinging his new shoes back and forth.

"Too bad," says Nell, "because it's a perfect day for digging and I have an extra trowel."
"No thanks," says Norman. "I'd rather watch."

Nell crouches down low.
Rusty crouches down low, too.

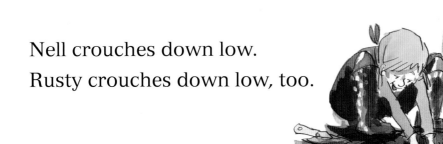

Sometimes Nell digs like a chipmunk and scratches out a little bit of dirt at a time.
Sometimes she's a badger and a lot of dirt flies everywhere!

And sometimes Nell closes her eyes and digs a tunnel like a mole.

But Rusty always digs like a dog. He uses his front paws to
make the hole deeper—and his back paws to put the dirt back in.
"Rusty!" scolds Nell, laughing.
Norman laughs, too, because he's not the one getting dirty.

Nell shapes a round mountain out of the first pile of dirt.
She decorates the mountain with pebbles and pieces of shells.
Rusty leaps over and over Nell's mountain until his paws are
the color of chocolate.

"**Ewww!**" says Norman, taking his clean hands out of the clean pockets of his clean jeans to keep the dirt away.

Nell has so much fun digging that she begins to dig another hole.
But Rusty has other ideas.
"Come back here!" calls Nell. "I'm going to catch you!"
Clomp! Clomp! Clomp! go Nell's digging boots in the swampy
spring mud.

"Hey! Stop splashing!" shouts Norman.
"Sorry," says Nell. "Good dog!" she tells Rusty because he's finally dropped the trowel.

This time when they dig, Nell and Rusty pretend they are giant steam shovels whirring, scooping, and dumping a ton of dirt next to each hole.

Then . . .

"Look what we found!" says Nell. "A pretty striped marble . . . three acorns . . . the mini stegosaurus I lost last summer and . . . one fat juicy worm!"

"**Gross!**" says Norman, but he inches closer to watch the worm wiggle, and to see what Nell decides to do with all the other treasures.

"We could put them in a dirt museum," Nell announces.
"**Cool!**" says Norman. "We'll build it with the stones
you dug up. And I won't even have to get dirty."

Nell makes sure to give the worm plenty of dirt to wiggle in.
Rusty wants to bite the worm, but Nell says, "Worms are not
for biting, Rusty. Mom says they make the garden better for
growing things like potatoes and tomatoes . . ."

"And flowers," says Norman.

Rusty thumps to the ground. He's pooped. But Nell—and
now Norman—want to see what else is buried in the garden.
So Norman brings Rusty a bowl of fresh water.

That does the trick!
"I still need your help,
partner," Nell tells Rusty.

When Nell and Rusty are digging their fifth hole,
Nell discovers something.
  "Hey Norman!" she calls.

"It's a tiny china arm!"

"Wow!" says Norman. He carefully brushes off the dirt
with his clean hankie. "I wonder who played with it—and if
there's more!"

"There's only one way to find out," says Nell. "But I'm all
dug out."

So . . .

Norman rolls up his
clean sleeves.

He rolls up the bottoms
of his clean jeans.

He picks up the
extra trowel.

And Norman starts to dig.

Not like a chipmunk and not like a badger. Not like a mole. And definitely not like a dog. Norman digs like a bird pecking away . . . slowly and carefully.

"If there's another treasure, I wouldn't want to break it," Norman says.

Then, just like an archaeologist, he separates the soil with the tip of his trowel, delicately spooning out a little dirt at a time, until . . .

Victory!

"Victory!" shouts Norman. "Could this be the tiny china leg
that goes with the tiny china arm that *you* found?"

"It is!" says Nell. "Good work, Norman. But guess what?"

"What?" asks Norman.

"You're all dirty!" says Nell.

"You're right," says Norman looking down. "But guess what?"

"What?" asks Nell.

"I *like* to dig!" says Norman. "And from now on my new shoes will be my digging shoes."

"But what about the garden?" asks Nell. "It's a mess!"
"*I know,*" says Norman. "We can fill in the holes like this . . ."

"And," says Nell, "we can plant these pansies like this . . . Hooray for digging!"

"You mean '**Hooray for dirty digging!**'" shouts Norman. "When can we dig again?"